Get Baking for the Holidays!

Get Baking for St. Patrick's Day!

By Ruth Owen

WINDMILL BOOKS

Published in 2023 by Windmill Books,
an Imprint of Rosen Publishing
29 East 21st Street, New York, NY 10010

Copyright © 2023 Windmill Books

All rights reserved. No part of this book may be reproduced in any form without permission in writing from the publisher, except by a reviewer.

Produced for Rosen by Ruth Owen Books

Designer
Emma Randall

Photos courtesy of Ruth Owen Books and Shutterstock

Cataloging-in-Publication Data
Names: Owen, Ruth.
Title: Get baking for St. Patrick's Day! / Ruth Owen.
Description: New York : Windmill Publishing, 2023. | Series: Get baking for the holidays | Includes glossary and index.
Identifiers: ISBN 9781508198321 (pbk.) | ISBN 9781508198345 (library bound) | ISBN 9781508198338 (6pack) | ISBN 9781508198352 (ebook)
Subjects: LCSH: Saint Patrick's Day--Juvenile literature. | Baking--Juvenile literature.
Classification: LCC GT4995.P3 O944 2023 | DDC 394.262--dc23

Printed in the United States of America

CPSIA Compliance Information: Batch CSWM23: For Further Information contact Rosen Publishing, New York, New York at 1-800-237-9932

Find us on

Contents

Get Ready to Bake 4

Lucky Cookies 6

Leprechaun Cupcakes 10

Nutty Green Muffins 14

Leprechaun Sharing Cookie 18

End of the Rainbow Cake 22

Treasure Pots Cupcakes 26

Glossary, Read More, Websites 30

Index 32

Get Ready to Bake

When St. Patrick's Day comes around, it's the perfect opportunity to head to the kitchen and get baking.

To bake the treats in this book you will need shamrock cookie cutters, sprinkles, and lots and lots of green food coloring! Before you get started check out all the tips on these pages to get the best results. Happy St. Patrick's Day!

Have Fun, Stay Safe!

It's very important to have an adult around whenever you do any of the following tasks in the kitchen:

- Using a mixer, the stovetop burners, or an oven.
- Using sharp utensils, such as knives and vegetable peelers or corers.
- Working with heated pans, pots, or baking sheets. Always use oven mitts when handling heated pans, pots, or baking sheets.

Measuring Counts

- Make sure you measure your ingredients carefully. If you get a measurement wrong, it could affect how successful your baking is.
- Use measuring scales or a measuring cup to measure dry and liquid ingredients.
- Measuring spoons can be used to measure small amounts of ingredients.

Measuring cup

Measuring spoons

Be Prepared
- Before cooking, always wash your hands well with soap and hot water.
- Make sure the kitchen countertop and all your equipment is clean.
- Read the recipe carefully before you start cooking. If you don't understand a step, ask an adult to help you.
- Gather together all the ingredients and equipment you will need. Baking is more fun when you're prepared!

REMEMBER:
Clean up the kitchen and put all your equipment away once you've finished baking.

Lucky Cookies

A green shamrock is one of the main **symbols** of the country of Ireland. A shamrock is also a symbol of St. Patrick's Day and is considered very lucky. Bake these buttery, sugary cookies as a treat for your family and friends and pass on some holiday luck!

Depending on the size of your cutter, these quantities will make up to 12 cookies.

Ingredients

To make the cookie dough:
- 1 ½ cups all-purpose flour (plus a little extra for dusting)
- ½ cup superfine sugar
- 5 ounces butter or margarine (plus a little for greasing)

For the frosting:
- ½ pound of green fondant
- A little powdered sugar for dusting
- Your choice of ready-to-use frosting pens or tubes
- Green Smarties, M&Ms, or sprinkles

Step 1 Grease the cookie sheets with a little butter to keep your cookies from sticking to the sheets.

Step 2 Put the butter and sugar into the mixing bowl and **cream together** with a spoon until smooth and fluffy.

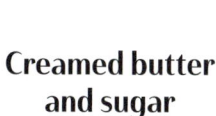

Creamed butter and sugar

Step 3 Add the flour and **beat** the mixture until the ingredients are blended and become crumbly. Next, use your hands to squeeze and **knead** the mixture to make a ball of soft dough.

Step 4 Wrap the dough in plastic wrap and place in a refrigerator for 30 minutes.

Dough

Equipment

- 2 large cookie sheets
- Mixing bowl
- Spoon for mixing
- Electric mixer (optional)
- Plastic wrap
- Rolling pin
- Shamrock-shaped cookie cutter
- Oven mitt
- Wire rack for cooling

Step 5 **Preheat** the oven to 350°F (180°C).

Step 6
Dust your countertop with a little flour. Unwrap the dough and place on the dusted surface. Roll out the dough to about ¼ inch (6 mm) thick.

Step 7
Cut as many shamrock shapes as you can from the dough and place them on the cookie sheets.

Greased cookie sheet

Step 8
Bake the cookies for about 15 minutes, or until they are turning golden. The centers of the cookies will still be slightly soft, but they'll soon firm up.

Using an oven mitt, remove the cookies from the oven. Allow to cool for about 10 minutes, and then carefully place each cookie on a wire rack and allow to cool completely.

Oven mitts

Step 9 Dust your countertop with a little powdered sugar. Take a small lump of fondant and roll out to about ¼ inch (6 mm) thick.

Cut shamrock shapes from the frosting for each cookie.

Step 10 Place the frosting shamrock on top of a cookie and smooth down the edges.

Step 11 Decorate the cookies with frosting patterns. You can also press green candies or decorations into the green frosting.

9

The quantities on this page will make 12 cupcakes..

Leprechaun Cupcakes

Ingredients

To make the cupcake batter:
- 7 ounces butter or margarine
- 1 cup superfine sugar
- 2 cups cake flour
- 1 teaspoon baking powder
- ¼ teaspoon salt
- 3 large eggs
- ½ teaspoon vanilla extract
- ½ cup milk

For the decorations and frosting:
- 2 ½ cups powdered sugar
- 1 cup butter
- 4 tablespoons milk
- Green food coloring
- Your choice of green and gold sprinkles and decorations
- Green fondant
- Tube of black frosting

Equipment

- 12-hole muffin pan
- 12 muffin cases
- Mixing bowl
- Wooden spoon
- Electric mixer (optional)
- Oven mitt
- Potholder
- Metal skewer
- Small bowl
- Spoon
- Frosting gun
- Small knife

Cupcakes are easy to make and great fun to decorate! Bake these delicious cakes and then get busy with oodles of green frosting, sprinkles, and other decorations. To make them into leprechaun-themed cupcakes, you can buy hat decorations online or from supermarkets, or follow our instructions to create your own mini fondant hats.

Step 1 Preheat the oven to 350°F (180°C).

Muffin pan

Step 2 Line the muffin pan with the muffin cases.

Muffin cases

Step 3 Put the butter and sugar into the mixing bowl and cream together with a wooden spoon until fluffy. If you wish, you can do this step using an electric mixer.

Step 4 Add the flour, baking powder, salt, eggs, milk, and vanilla extract to the bowl. Use a wooden spoon or electric mixer to beat the ingredients together until the mixture is thick and smooth.

Step 5 Spoon the mixture into the muffin cases, sharing it equally.

Cupcake batter

11

Step 6 Bake the cakes for 20 minutes, or until they have risen above the edges of the muffin cases. To test if the cakes are baked, insert a metal skewer into one cake. If it comes out clean, the cakes are ready.

Step 7 Using an oven mitt, remove the muffin pan from the oven and set it on a potholder. Allow the cakes to cool completely.

Baked cupcakes

Step 8 To make the frosting, mix the powdered sugar, butter, and milk together in a small bowl until thick and smooth.

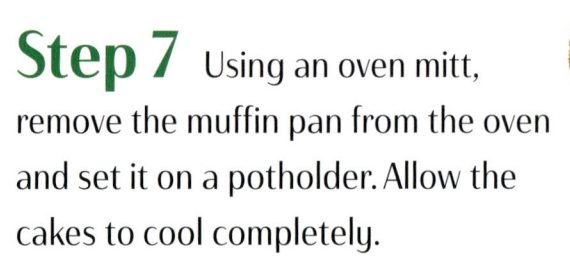

Step 9 Carefully add drops of green food coloring into the bowl, mixing to get the frosting color you want.

Frosting gun

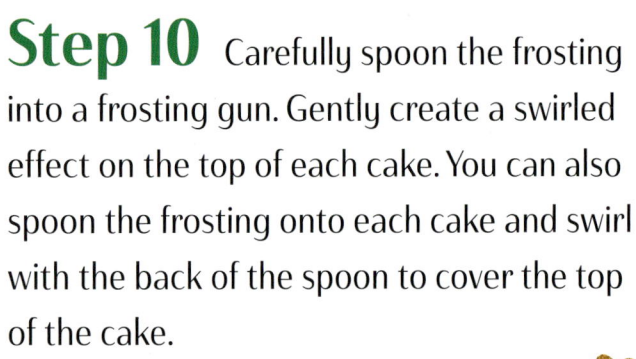

Step 10 Carefully spoon the frosting into a frosting gun. Gently create a swirled effect on the top of each cake. You can also spoon the frosting onto each cake and swirl with the back of the spoon to cover the top of the cake.

Step 11
Add sprinkles and other decorations.

Step 12
To make a leprechaun hat, take some green fondant and roll it into a sausage-like tube.

Cut a small section of the tube to be the top of the hat.

Make a small ball of frosting and flatten it into a circle to make the bottom of the hat. Press the top and bottom parts together.

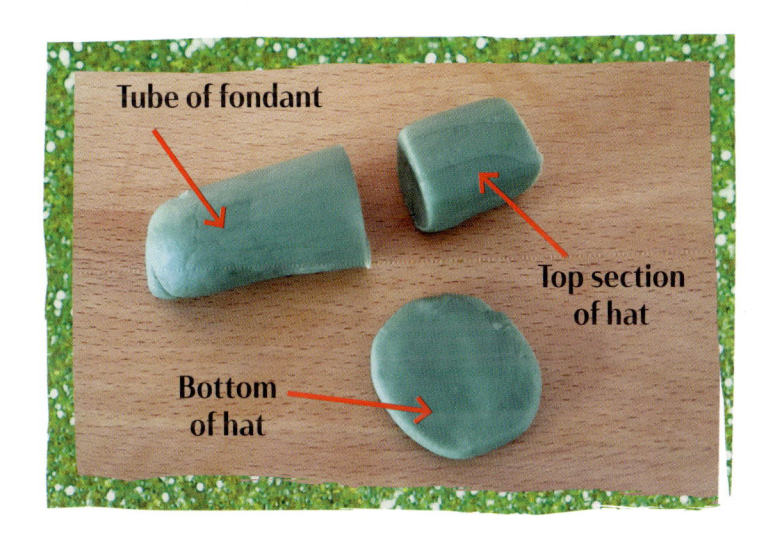

Tube of fondant

Top section of hat

Bottom of hat

Draw a band around the hat with black frosting and add a gold decoration for a buckle.

Happy St. Patrick's Day!

Nutty Green Muffins

Add some pistachios and green food coloring to your muffin mixture to create some celebratory bakes that are just right for this holiday. Bake your muffins in advance of the big day, or serve them warm from the oven to your St. Patrick's Day guests.

The quantities on this page will make 10 muffins.

Ingredients

- 1 ⅓ cups all-purpose flour
- 2 teaspoons baking powder
- ½ teaspoon salt
- ½ teaspoon ground cinnamon
- ¼ teaspoon nutmeg
- 1 small lemon
- 1 cup finely chopped pistachios
- ½ cup butter or margarine (plus a little extra for greasing)
- ⅔ cup granulated sugar
- 2 large eggs
- 1 teaspoon vanilla extract
- ½ cup milk
- Green food coloring gel

Step 1 Preheat the oven to 425°F (220°C).

Step 2 Grease the muffin pan with a little butter to keep the muffins from sticking.

Chopped pistachios

Step 3 Place the flour, baking powder, salt, cinnamon, nutmeg, and half the pistachios into the first mixing bowl and mix thoroughly with a wooden spoon.

Step 4 Wash the lemon and then **zest**, or finely grate, the rind of the lemon. Add 1 teaspoon of lemon zest to the bowl and mix.

Step 5 Put the butter and sugar into the second mixing bowl and cream together with a wooden spoon until fluffy. If you wish, you can use an electric mixer for this step.

Equipment

- 1 12-hole or 2 6-hole muffin pans
- 2 mixing bowls
- Wooden spoon
- Grater
- Electric mixer (optional)
- Oven mitts
- Potholder
- Metal skewer
- Wire rack for cooling

Step 6 Add the eggs to the creamed butter and sugar and beat the mixture until light and fluffy. Add the vanilla extract and gently stir in.

Step 7 Now add about a quarter of the dry flour mixture and a quarter of the milk to the mixture of butter, sugar, and eggs. Mix together with a wooden spoon or electric mixer until combined. Do not **overmix** the ingredients.

Step 8 Repeat step 7 until all the ingredients are mixed together.

Green food coloring gel

Step 9 If you wish to add green coloring, do this now. Stir in a tiny blob of gel coloring about half the size of a pinkie fingernail. Remember, you can always add more coloring to get the correct color, but if you add too much at the start, you can't remove it!

Step 10 Spoon the mixture equally between 10 muffin pan sections. Sprinkle the remaining pistachios over the top.

Step 11 Place the muffins in the oven and immediately turn down the temperature to 375°F (190°C).

Step 12 Bake the muffins for 15 minutes. To test if the muffins are baked, insert a metal skewer into one muffin. If it comes out clean, the muffins are ready.

Step 13 Place the muffin pan on a potholder to cool for about five minutes. Then carefully lift each muffin from the pan. Eat while hot, or stand the muffins on a wire rack to cool.

17

> The quantities on this page will make 2 dinner plate-sized cookies.

Leprechaun Sharing Cookie

Leprechauns are tiny fairy folk with bushy orange beards and green suits. They appear in lots of Irish **legends**. To ensure a leprechaun joins your St. Patrick's Day celebrations, make this giant chocolate chip cookie and then use frosting to give your sharing cookie a funny leprechaun face.

Ingredients

To make the cookie dough:
- 1 ½ sticks of butter (plus a little extra for greasing)
- 1 ½ cups superfine sugar
- 1 cup light brown sugar
- 2 eggs
- 2 teaspoons vanilla extract
- 3 cups cake flour
- 1 teaspoon salt
- 1 cup chocolate chips

For the decorations and frosting:
- 2 ½ cups powdered sugar
- 1 cup butter
- 4 tablespoons milk
- Green and orange food coloring
- Tube of black frosting
- Yellow and brown candies

Equipment

- 2 cookie sheets
- Large mixing bowl
- Wooden spoon
- Electric mixer (optional)
- Small bowl
- Hand whisk
- Sieve
- Oven mitts
- 2 potholders
- 2 small bowls (for frosting)
- Spoons for mixing frosting
- Rubber spatula
- Frosting gun

18

Step 1 Preheat the oven to 350°F (180°C).

Step 2 Grease the two cookie sheets with a little butter.

Step 3 To make the cookie dough, put the butter and sugars into the mixing bowl and cream together with a wooden spoon until fluffy. If you wish, you can use an electric mixer for this step.

Step 4 Break the eggs into the small bowl and then beat them with a hand whisk.

Step 5 Pour the eggs and vanilla extract into the mixing bowl. Beat all the ingredients in the bowl together with a wooden spoon until they are combined.

Step 6 Sift the flour and salt into the mixing bowl and then stir into the other ingredients with the wooden spoon.

Step 7 Add the chocolate chips and stir through the dough.

Chocolate chip cookie dough

Step 8 Divide the cookie dough in two and form it into two balls. If the dough is wet and sticky, place in a refrigerator for about 30 minutes so it firms up.

Step 9 Place each ball of dough on a cookie sheet. Then flatten and squeeze the dough with your hands to form a dinner plate-sized cookie that's about ½ inch (1.25 cm) thick.

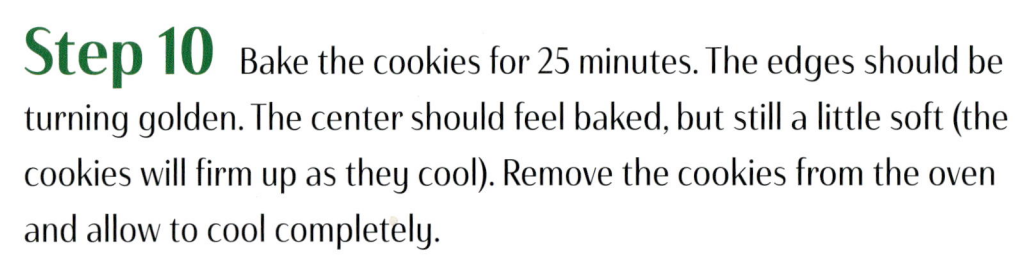

Step 10 Bake the cookies for 25 minutes. The edges should be turning golden. The center should feel baked, but still a little soft (the cookies will firm up as they cool). Remove the cookies from the oven and allow to cool completely.

Step 11 To make the frosting, mix the powdered sugar, butter, and milk together in a bowl until thick and smooth.

Step 12 Divide the frosting in half and then put a teaspoon of frosting to one side. Color half the frosting green and half orange.

Spatula

Step 13 Use a spatula or the back of a spoon to smear green icing over the top third of a cookie.

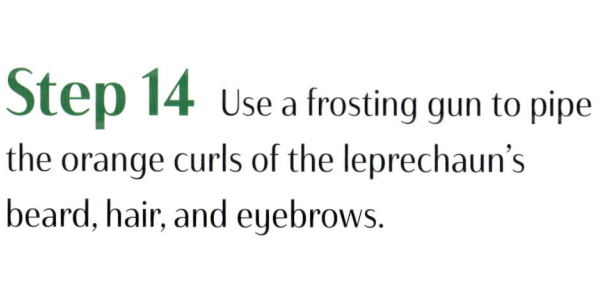

Step 14 Use a frosting gun to pipe the orange curls of the leprechaun's beard, hair, and eyebrows.

A buckle made of yellow candies

Black band of frosting

Candy eyes

Blob of frosting for a pointed nose

Black frosting mouth

Step 15 Use candies, black frosting, and the blob of uncolored frosting to complete the decorations.

21

The quantities on this page will make one large frosted cake with six layers.

End of the Rainbow Cake

Ingredients

To make the cake batter:
- 3 cups cake flour
- 3 teaspoons baking powder
- 12 ounces soft, unsalted butter (plus extra for greasing)
- 2 cups superfine sugar
- 6 large eggs
- 1 tablespoon vanilla extract
- ¼ cup milk
- Red, orange, yellow, green, blue, and purple food coloring gel

To make the frosting:
- 5 ounces butter
- 13 ounces cream cheese
- 7 ½ cups powdered sugar
- Rainbow-colored sprinkles (optional)

Equipment

- 2 7-inch cake pans
- 2 mixing bowls
- Wooden spoon
- Electric mixer (optional)
- 6 small bowls
- Spoons for mixing
- Rubber spatula
- Oven mitts
- Potholder
- Metal skewer
- Wire rack for cooling
- A plate for serving
- Serrated knife

This amazing (and easy-to-make) rainbow layer cake is just perfect for St. Patrick's Day. Why? It's said that a leprechaun tells humans that he's hidden a pot of gold at the end of the rainbow. Of course, it's just a trick because everyone knows it's impossible to find the end of a rainbow!

You can buy rainbow gel food coloring kits online. Read the customer reviews to make sure you are buying products that achieve true, bright colors once the cakes are baked.

Step 1 Grease the two cake pans with a little butter to keep your cakes from sticking. You will be baking the six layers two at a time.

Step 2 Put the butter and sugar into a mixing bowl and cream together with a wooden spoon until fluffy. If you wish, you can do this step using an electric mixer. Add the eggs to the mixture one at a time and gently beat into the mixture.

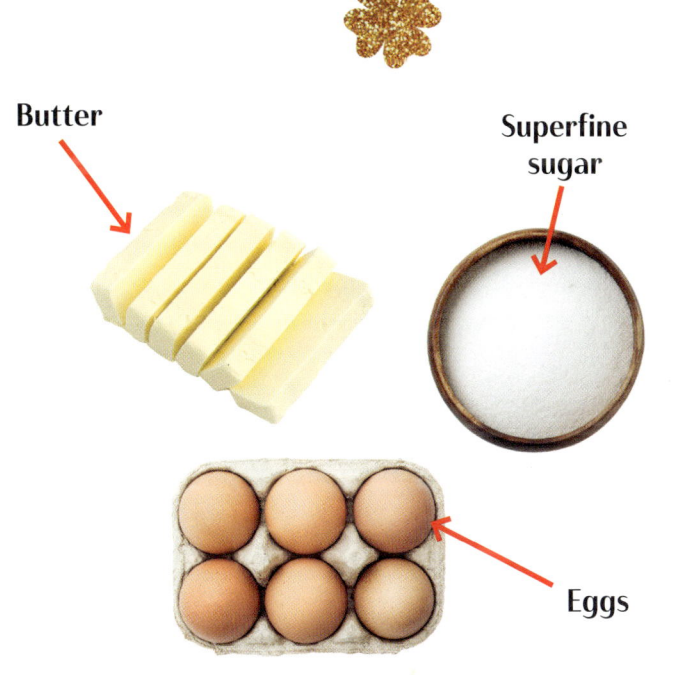

Butter

Superfine sugar

Eggs

Step 3 Add the flour, baking powder, and vanilla extract and beat until thoroughly combined. The mixture should be a thick liquid. If it's a little stiff and won't pour, add a little of the milk.

Cake flour

Vanilla extract

Step 4 Preheat the oven to 350°F (180°C).

Step 5 Divide the mixture equally between the six small bowls.

23

Step 6 Now add a different food coloring to each bowl. Add the gel in a tiny blob (about half the size of your pinkie fingernail). Keep adding until you have a strong, bright color.

Rainbow gel food colorings

Cake pan

Batter

Step 7 Use a spatula to scoop one bowl of batter into a cake pan. Then add a different color of batter to the second cake pan. Smooth the top of the batter with a spatula.

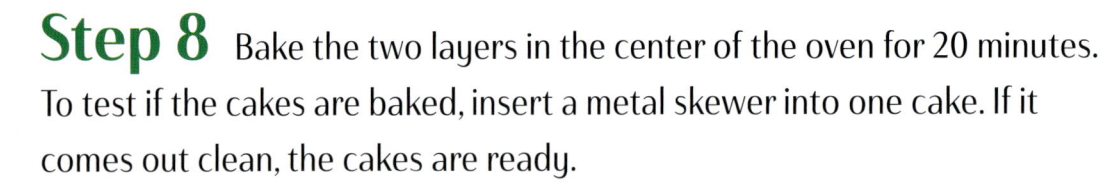

Step 8 Bake the two layers in the center of the oven for 20 minutes. To test if the cakes are baked, insert a metal skewer into one cake. If it comes out clean, the cakes are ready.

Step 9 Carefully remove the cakes from the pan and place on a wire rack to cool.
Don't worry if your cakes look a little dark. This is just a little browning from the butter in the pans. The colors inside will be fresh and bright.

Step 10 Wash and re-grease the pans and then repeat steps 7 to 9 until all six layers are baked and thoroughly cooled.

Step 11 To make the frosting, mix the powdered sugar, butter, and cream cheese together until thick and smooth.

Step 12 To assemble the cake, place the purple layer on the serving plate. If the cake has risen unevenly or is slightly domed, carefully use a serrated knife to slice off any high points and create a flat surface. Smear on a layer of frosting with a spatula.

Step 13 Place the blue layer on top of the frosting. Keep adding the layers with frosting sandwiched between them.

This yellow layer has been trimmed to create a flat surface.

Slightly browned edges

Step 14 Once the final layer (red) is in place, smear a layer of frosting on top of the cake. Carefully use a spatula to smear frosting over the sides of the cake, too. You should use about half of the frosting. Put the cake in the refrigerator to help the frosting firm up.

You can add rainbow sprinkles.

Step 15 Later, or the next day, add the remaining frosting to the top and sides of the cake until it is evenly covered.

Enjoy!

Treasure Pots Cupcakes

The quantities on this page will make 12 cupcakes.

Ingredients

To make the cake batter:
- 7 ounces butter or margarine
- 1 cup superfine sugar
- 2 cups cake flour
- 1 teaspoon baking powder
- ¼ teaspoon salt
- 3 large eggs
- ½ cup milk
- ½ teaspoon vanilla extract

For the decorations and frosting:
- 2 ½ cups powdered sugar
- 1 cup butter
- 4 tablespoons milk
- Your choice of food colorings, sprinkles, and other candies

Equipment

- 12-hole muffin pan
- 12 muffin cases
- Mixing bowl
- Wooden spoon
- Electric mixer (optional)
- Oven mitts
- Metal skewer
- Potholder
- Wire rack for cooling
- Small bowls
- Spoons for mixing
- Small knife

When someone bites into one of these cupcakes or cuts it open, they will get a surprise as treasure spills from the cake! Leprechaun pots of gold are a popular St. Patrick's Day theme. So make these colorful cupcakes that are mini pots of treasure, packed with gold sprinkles and other candies. These cakes make a great holiday gift or are perfect to serve to your guests on the big day.

Step 1 Preheat the oven to 350°F (180°C).

Step 2 Line the muffin pan with muffin cases.

Step 3 Put the butter and sugar into the mixing bowl and cream together with a wooden spoon until fluffy. If you wish, you can use an electric mixer for this step.

Step 4 Add the flour, baking powder, salt, eggs, milk, and vanilla extract to the bowl. Use a wooden spoon or electric mixer to beat the ingredients together until the mixture is thick and smooth.

Cupcake batter

Step 5 Spoon the mixture into the muffin cases, sharing it equally.

Step 6
Bake the cakes for 20 minutes, or until they have risen above the edges of the muffin cases. To test if the cakes are baked, insert a metal skewer into one cake. If it comes out clean, the cakes are ready.

Step 7
Stand the muffin pan on a potholder and carefully remove the cakes from the pan, standing them on a wire rack to cool.

Step 8
To make the frosting, mix the powdered sugar, butter, and milk together until thick and smooth.

Step 9
Divide the frosting between several small bowls. Carefully add small amounts of food coloring to each bowl to get the frosting colors you want.

Wedge-shaped core

Step 10
Take a cupcake and cut a small, wedge-shaped core from the cake.

Fill the inside of the cake with your choice of gold sprinkles and other candies.

28

Step 11 Trim off the top part of the core and use it to plug the hole in the top of the cake.

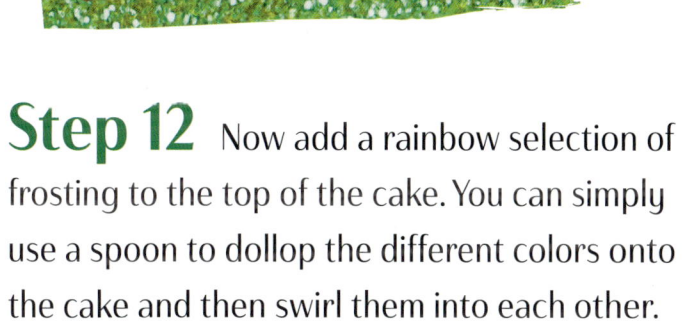

Step 12 Now add a rainbow selection of frosting to the top of the cake. You can simply use a spoon to dollop the different colors onto the cake and then swirl them into each other. Finally, add some rainbow sprinkles.

Have a great St. Patrick's Day!

Glossary

beat
To blend a mixture of ingredients until they are smooth with equipment such as a spoon, fork, hand whisk, or electric mixer.

cream together
To beat butter or margarine, usually with sugar, to make it light and fluffy.

knead
To press, squeeze, and fold dough with your hands to make it smooth and stretchy.

legends
Stories handed down from long ago that are often based on some facts but cannot be proven to be true.

overmix
Mixing a dough or batter too much. When flour is exposed to liquid and stirred, the gluten in the flour starts developing into a network that binds all the ingredients together. If too much mixing takes place, the gluten can develop too much and cause the baked goods to become tough. Only mix flour and other ingredients until they are combined and then stop.

preheat
To turn on an oven so it is at the correct temperature for cooking a particular dish before the food is placed inside.

symbols
Objects or pictures that stand for or represent another thing, such as an important event or person. For example, a shamrock may be a symbol of St. Patrick's Day.

zest
The brightly colored outer part of the rind of citrus fruits, such as lemons and oranges. Also, the word used to describe grating the zest of a fruit so it can be used in cooking.

Read More

Owen, Ruth. *Celebrations and Special Days (My World Your World)*. Minneapolis, MN: Ruby Tuesday Books, 2015.

Owen, Ruth. *Kids Cook (Creative Kids)*. New York: Windmill Books, 2017.

Owen, Ruth. *Let's Celebrate with St. Patrick's Day Origami (Let's Celebrate with Origami)*. New York: Enslow Publishing, 2022.

Websites

https://www.tasteofhome.com/collection/st-patricks-day-recipes-for-kids//

https://kids.nationalgeographic.com/celebrations/article/st-patricks-day

https://www.activityvillage.co.uk/st-patricks-day-crafts

Publisher's note to educators and parents: Our editors have carefully reviewed these websites to ensure that they are suitable for students. Many websites change frequently, however, and we cannot guarantee that a site's future contents will continue to meet our high standards of quality and educational value. Be advised that students should be closely supervised whenever they access the internet.

Index

E

end of the rainbow cake, 22-23, 24-25

F

frosting & decorating, 9, 12-13, 21, 25, 28-29

H

hygiene, 5

L

leprechaun cookies, 10-11, 12-13
leprechaun sharing cookies, 18-19, 20-21
lucky cookies, 6-7, 8-9

M

measuring, 4

N

nutty green muffins, 14-15, 16-17

S

safety, 4

T

treasure pots cookies, 26-27, 28-29